These books have been
purchased for the library system
with donations by the
Youngsville Elementary School
Kindergarten Pennies Program.

THE
BABY BUNNY

Modern Curriculum Press
**BEGINNING
TO
READ**
Series

THE BABY BUNNY

Margaret Hillert

Illustrated by Robert Masheris

MODERN CURRICULUM PRESS

ISBN: 0-8136-5564-1
Printed in the United States of America

17 18 19 20 21 22 ᐧ   06 05 04 03 02

Pearson Learning Group

1-800-321-3106
www.pearsonlearning.com

Here is a baby.

Is it a bunny?

No, it is not a bunny.

Here is a baby.
Is it a bunny?
No, it is not a bunny.

Where is the baby bunny?
Do you see it now?
Look, look.
Can you find it?

7

Oh, yes.

Here it is.

Down in here.

And here is the mother, too.

What a little baby it is.
Can it run?
Can it jump?
No, no.
It is too little.

The bunny wants to eat.
See what the mother can do.
The mother can help.

The mother can do this, too.
See the mother work.
The bunny likes it.

Now see the baby bunny.
It is not too little.
It can come out here.

It can run.
It can jump.
It can play.

Look, look.

The bunny can find something.

The bunny can eat and eat and eat.

15

And look now.
See what the bunny can do.
This is good.

What will the bunny do now?
Where will the bunny go?
Can you guess?

17

Away, away.
Up,
    and up,
       and up.

Down,
    down,
        down,
            down,
                down.

What is this?

What can the bunny see?

It looks like the little bunny.

Here is something funny.

It can not run.

It can not run at the bunny.

What will it do?
It will go away now.
Away, away.

25

Here comes something.
Something big.
Look out, little bunny.
Look out.

Run, run, run.
Get away.
Get away, little bunny.

Oh, here is the mother.
This is good.
The mother can help.

Look at this.
Look in here.
The baby is with the mother.
No one can get the baby bunny now.

31

Margaret Hillert, author and poet, has written many books for young readers. She is a former first-grade teacher and lives in Birmingham, Michigan.

The Baby Bunny uses the 51 words listed below.

a	get	mother	the
and	go		this
at	good	no	to
away	guess	not	too
		now	
baby	help		up
big	here	oh	
bunny		one	want(s)
	in	out	what
can	is		where
come(s)	it	play	will
			with
do	jump	run	work
down			
	likes	see	yes
eat	little	something	you
	look(s)		
find			
funny			